Tooth Trouble

Tooth Trouble

by ABBY KLEIN

illustrated by
JOHN MCKINLEY

SCHOLASTIC INC.
New York   Toronto   London   Auckland   Sydney
Mexico City   New Delhi   Hong Kong   Buenos Aires

To Mouse, Toes, and my Sweet Pea—
thank you for believing in me!
I love you guys.
—A. K.

This book is being published simultaneously in hardcover
by the Blue Sky Press.

ISBN 0-439-55596-5

Text copyright © 2004 by Abby Klein
Illustrations copyright © 2004 by John McKinley

Special thanks to Robert Martin Staenberg.

12   8 9/0

Printed in the United States of America   40

First Scholastic paperback printing, August 2004

CHAPTERS

I have a problem.

A really, really, big problem.

I'm the only one in my class

who hasn't lost a tooth.

Let me tell you about it.

CHAPTER 1

The Only One

Today when the bell rang at the end of recess, my best friend, Robbie, came running into the classroom and almost knocked me over.

"Hey, watch it!" I said.

Robbie was jumping up and down and waving his hands in the air, shouting, "I lost my tooth! I lost my tooth!" He was holding the tooth between his fingers, and he stuck his arm high in the air so everybody could see.

"Let *me* see," said Jessie.

Robbie smiled really wide and, sure enough, there was a big, bloody hole where his baby tooth used to be.

"*Eewww,*" said Chloe, backing up. "That is *disgusting*! Get away from me! You're going to get blood on my brand-new velvet dress."

"Is there a lot of blood?" Robbie asked, smiling.

Just then Mrs. Wushy, our teacher, came over and said, "Oh, it's just a little bit of blood. Why don't you go over to the sink and rinse your mouth out with water? Just swish and spit, but don't swallow."

"Yeah, blood is cool," said Jessie, "but you don't want to drink it. You'll get a stomachache."

"Actually, blood is mostly water,"

said Robbie, "so it really won't hurt you." Robbie is a science genius. He's read about a million books, and he knows everything about everything.

"But only Dracula actually drinks blood," I said.

"And so does Mr. Pendergast," Max said, laughing. Mr. Pendergast, in case you don't know, is our principal. We call him The Skunk. His hair is black, except for a thin gray stripe that runs right down the middle, but that's not why we call him The Skunk. We call him The Skunk because his breath stinks. Whenever he talks to you, you think you're going to pass out from the smell.

"Here's a bag to put your tooth in, Robbie, so you don't lose it," said Mrs. Wushy, holding up a plastic sandwich bag.

"You have to keep it safe so you can put it under your pillow tonight for the Tooth Fairy. Once you're finished, then come to the rug, and you can sign the Big Tooth."

The Big Tooth. I hate that Big Tooth. Mrs. Wushy puts up a new tooth every month, and you get to write your name on this big paper tooth every time your tooth falls out.

Jessie "Nothin' Scares Me" Sanchez got to sign her name on there twice.

Max "The Meanie" Sellars went up to sign his name for the third time last week. And Chloe "I'm So Wonderful" Winters has written her name on there four times already this year.

I haven't gotten to sign my name even one lousy time.

"Great, just great," I mumbled. "My dumb old teeth don't want to come out."

Before today, Robbie and I were the only ones who hadn't lost a tooth yet.

Now I'm the only one.

The only one who hasn't lost a tooth!

"Everyone, please come to the rug," said Mrs. Wushy. "It's time for Robbie to sign the tooth."

"Whoop-de-doo for him," I muttered. "Let's have a party."

Robbie strutted proudly up to the front of the room.

"Here you go, Robbie," said Mrs. Wushy, handing him the special pen with the smiling tooth on top.

Robbie took the pen and signed his name. REALLY BIG. R-O-B-B-I-E.

"Congratulations," said Mrs. Wushy, and everyone clapped loudly for Robbie. Well, everyone except me.

"Now let's see," said Mrs. Wushy, as she pointed at our tooth graph. "It looks like Freddy Thresher is the only one who hasn't lost a tooth yet."

Great! Did she have to announce it to the whole class?

Now everyone was staring at me, and I think a couple of kids were laughing.

I was *soooo* embarrassed. My face got as red as a tomato. I wished I could make myself invisible.

"Uh, can I go to the bathroom?" I asked Mrs. Wushy.

"Sure," she said.

I didn't walk. I bolted to the bathroom. I just wanted to get out of there.

When I was safe inside the bathroom, I first checked to make sure no one else was in there, and then I looked in the mirror and smiled, really big.

"HEY, WOULD JUST ONE OF YOU STUPID TEETH COME OUT ALREADY?!!" I yelled.

I decided right then and there that no matter what, I was going to lose a tooth. And soon.

I just had to come up with a plan.

CHAPTER 2

Five Ways
to Lose a Tooth

That night I didn't feel like eating any dinner.

"What's wrong with you?" my mom asked. "You haven't touched your food."

"I'm not hungry," I mumbled.

"Not hungry?" said my mom. "But it's your favorite—tuna noodle casserole. You must be getting sick. I'll go and get the thermometer."

"I'M NOT SICK!" I shouted.

"Oooh, somebody's in a yucky mood," said my big sister, Suzie.

"Be quiet!" I yelled. I lunged toward Suzie to pull her hair, but I slipped, and my elbow fell right into her plate—sending a pile of tuna noodle sailing to the floor.

"Hey, hey, stop it, you two!" said my dad. My dad can be a pretty serious guy, and if he says stop, you'd better stop if you know what's good for you.

"Look at the mess you made!" said my mom as she ran to get a sponge. She's such a Neat Freak. Our floors are so clean you could eat off them.

"I'm not sick. I just had a bad day at school today," I whispered.

"Oh, did the little first grader pee in his pants?" teased my sister. "Or did somebody

21

spill milk on one of your dumb old shark shirts?"

"LEAVE ME ALONE, YOU DING-DONG STINKY HEAD!" I shouted back. "For your information, I am a shark expert, and they are not dumb. Sharks are cool. You're just jealous of all my cool shark stuff."

"I am not, Brat!" Suzie yelled back.

"Please, Suzie," said my mom, wiping the floor. "Just leave him alone. He's upset about something, and you're not helping." She gave Suzie one of her all-time famous Shut-Your-Mouth-Now Death Stares. "Now, Freddy, tell us what's bothering you."

"I'm the only one," I said, sniffling.

"What do you mean, 'the only one'?" asked my dad.

"Robbie lost his tooth today, so now I'm

the only one in my class who hasn't lost a tooth."

"You want to lose a tooth?" said my sister. "Why didn't you just say so? I can help you with that."

"Really?" I said, my face brightening.

"Sure. In fact, I'll show you *five* ways to lose a tooth." Then she held up her right hand and bent her fingers down one at a time as she counted, "One, two, three, four, five," until her hand was making a fist.

"Come on over here, and I'll punch you in the mouth. That should knock a few of those teeth loose," she said, laughing hysterically.

"Oh, Suzie, that's so funny I forgot to laugh," I said.

"Suzie Marie Thresher, that is ENOUGH!" said my dad. "I think you need to go to your room right now."

"I don't want to!"

"I didn't ask you. I'm telling you. Now let's go."

After the two of them left the kitchen, my mom came over and put her arm around me. "Don't worry, baby," she said, kissing the top of my head. "One of those little teeth will get loose sooner or later. Just be patient."

"I don't want to be patient!" I cried, pulling away. I ran to my room and slammed the door.

Then I stopped, dead in my tracks. Because I just got a great idea.

CHAPTER 3

The Door Disaster

Slamming the door reminded me of this *Commander Upchuck* episode I saw one time on TV.

Commander Upchuck had this really bad toothache.

His tooth hurt so bad he wanted to get it out, so he asked his friend, Cookie, what he should do.

Cookie got a string and tied one end of the string to Commander Upchuck's tooth and the other end to a door. Then he slammed the door a bunch of times, and *BOOM!* the tooth came out.

"Hey, why didn't I think of that before?" I said to myself.

I was so excited! I ran to my treasure box, dumped it on the floor, and started digging through my stuff. I found my Commander Upchuck fan club membership card, the two-dollar bill my grandpa gave me for my birthday, my hammerhead magnet from the aquarium, the plastic sword and mini umbrella from my fancy drink at the grown-up restaurant, my shark's tooth necklace, and my dad's cool business card. (He's a producer on the kids' TV show *Fun Factory*.)

Then I saw it. The string I found on the playground last week. Great! I knew it would come in handy. Now I needed some tape. I'm not very good at tying. In fact, I can hardly even tie my own shoes, so tape would make the job a lot easier.

I scanned my room for the roll of tape I borrowed from my mom and spotted it in my fishbowl. What on earth was it doing in there? Oh yeah, now I remember.

I was pretending it was a hoop, and I was trying to train my goldfish, Mako, to swim through it, just like the dolphins at Wet 'n Wild. I really want a dog because you can teach them to do lots of cool tricks, but my mom says a dog is too dirty, and it would destroy the house. What does she think a dog is—Godzilla?

I pulled the tape out of the fishbowl and dried it on my pillowcase. As I started

taping the string to my doorknob, my
sister came running down the hall and
pounded on my door.

I jumped back.

"Hey, Shark Bait!" she yelled. "I'm doing
my homework, and I can't find my pencil
sharpener. Did you take it?" she asked,
trying to push my door open.

Oh no! I couldn't let her in. If she saw

me using my mom's tape on the doorknob, she'd tell on me, and then I'd really be in big trouble.

I leaned on the door as hard as I could and yelled, "Go away, Dog Breath! I don't have your dumb pencil sharpener."

"Hey, let me in, Chubby Cheeks," she demanded. "What are you doing in there, anyway?"

"Nothing, you big pain. Now go away."

"You must be up to something if you won't let me in. I'm telling. Mom, Dad! Freddy's up to something!" she called as her footsteps disappeared down the hall.

Now I really had to hurry. I didn't want my parents to see what I was doing, or I'd get in BIG trouble for two reasons. One, I was only supposed to use her tape for special art projects. Two, my mom, The Clean Machine, would go nuts if I actually did yank my tooth out and got blood all over the carpet.

I didn't care. I had to get my name on that Big Tooth. I picked up the string, wrapped it around my tooth a couple of times, and tried to tape the end to the front of my tooth.

"Oh, come on, come on, you stupid string," I muttered under my breath.

The string and tape were both getting all wet and slimy from my spit, and they kept slipping out of my fingers.

I pulled some of the string out of my mouth and looked at it.

It had a gooey chunk of tuna noodle casserole from dinner stuck to the end. I licked it off and tried to tape the string on to my tooth again.

Just then there was another knock on my door. "Honey, what are you doing?"

I gulped. It was my mother. I grabbed

the string and tape and tried to yank it out, but it was stuck! The string had gotten caught between my teeth!

"Freddy, are you all right?"

"Uh-huh."

"I can't hear you. What did you say?" She started to turn the knob.

"See?" said my sister. "I told you he was up to something."

Oh no! I couldn't let them see me tied to the doorknob like this. My mother would go crazy and I'd never hear the end of it from Suzie. I ripped the end of the string off the doorknob and shoved the whole thing, tape and all, into my mouth just as my mom pushed the door open.

"What's going on in here?"

"Nummin," I mumbled, trying not to open my overstuffed mouth.

She looked around my room. "Why is the stuff from your treasure box all over the floor? Did you make this mess?"

"Ugmmm, ugmmmm," I answered, shaking my head.

"Well then, who did? The boogeyman? Freddy, how many times have I told you not to make a big mess right before bed-time? You have two minutes to put every-thing away, mister, or no TV tomorrow. Do I make myself clear?"

"Mmmmm, mmmmm." I nodded.

"I mean it. Two minutes."

"Ommm-kayyy," I said, trying not to open my mouth.

"Not very talkative tonight, are you? Are you still upset about not losing a tooth?"

I wished she would leave already. I was

going to swallow the string and choke to death if she stayed a minute longer.

"Don't worry. I didn't lose my first tooth until *I* was in first grade." She smiled.

"Now hop to it. You've got two minutes to clean up this mess, and then I'll be back to give you a kiss good night."

She left, and I finally spit the slimy, sticky, soaked wad of tape and string out of my mouth.

Whew, that was a close one.

Since the doorknob plan required tying, and I probably couldn't even learn to tie my own shoes in less than a week, I was going to have to come up with another plan. I squeezed my lucky shark tooth. If I squeeze it hard enough, a good idea pops into my head, but nothing was popping in there tonight.

I lay down on my bed and hit my forehead with the palm of my hand. "Think, think, think," I said.

CHAPTER 4

Plan B

The next day at school was even worse! Everywhere I went, all that the kids talked about was teeth, teeth, TEETH!

During math time, Jessie asked Robbie, "Did the Tooth Fairy come to your house last night?"

"Yeah," said Robbie, his eyes lighting up.

"What did she leave you?"

"I put my tooth under my pillow when

I went to sleep, and in the morning, the tooth was gone, and the Tooth Fairy left me a dollar bill!"

"One dollar? Is that *all*?" said Chloe, wrinkling up her nose. "The Tooth Fairy gives me *five* dollars."

"Five dollars!" said Jessie. "You're rich!"

"I know," said Chloe, playing with her shiny, gold necklace and flashing her million-dollar smile. "Since I already lost four teeth, I have twenty whole dollars."

"My *abuela*, you know, my grandma, well, she's really good at sewing, so she made me a little tooth pillow," said Jessie. "It looks like a smile, and there's a little pocket where the missing tooth goes. The Tooth Fairy leaves a shiny silver dollar in the little pocket. I'm saving up for a new

skateboard like the one you got for your birthday, Freddy."

"How 'bout you, Freddy?" said Chloe. "What does the Tooth Fairy bring you?"

Before I could answer, Max butted in and said, "A big, fat, nothin'! The Tooth Fairy has never been to Freddy's house, remember? Freddy's just a baby. He hasn't lost a tooth yet."

"Well, she'll be coming soon," I said, "'cause I have a really loose tooth."

"Oh yeah?" said Max. "Which one? Show me, Shark Boy!"

"I don't have to show you."

"Liar!" said Max. "You don't have a loose tooth."

"Do too!"

"Do not!"

"Do too!"

"Do not!"

"Boys, what is the problem here?" Mrs. Wushy interrupted. "What is all this yelling about?"

"Nothin'," I mumbled, looking down at the ground.

"Oh, nothin', Mrs. Wushy. We were just talkin'," said Max.

"Well, I need to see a lot less talking and

a lot more working," Mrs. Wushy said. "You both need to finish that page of math problems before recess."

As soon as Mrs. Wushy walked away, Max smiled and whispered, "We'll finish this conversation at recess, wimp."

Oh great. Just great. I was going to get beat up by the meanest kid in the class. No . . . correction . . . the biggest bully in the whole first grade.

My stomach started doing flips. I was sure I was going to throw up.

"Uh . . . Mrs. Wushy . . . may I go to the bathroom?"

"Are you feeling okay, Freddy? You look a little pale."

"I'm, uh, fine. I just need to go."

"Well, go ahead then."

I ran to the bathroom, went into one of

the stalls, locked the door, and sat down on the toilet to think.

Why did I talk back to Max Sellars, the biggest bully in the whole first grade? He was going to squish me like a bug.

I hit my forehead with the palm of my hand. Think, think, think . . .

I'm going to get beat up by the bully.

He's gonna smush me!

He's gonna crush me!

He's gonna rip me to pieces like a great white shark snacking on a tuna fish!

He's gonna turn my face into oatmeal!

I hit my head harder. Think, think, think . . .

Wait a minute. . . . I'm going to get beat up by the bully! This is my lucky day!

He's gonna smush me!

He's gonna crush me!

He's gonna rip me to pieces!

He's gonna turn my face into oatmeal!

He's gonna knock my tooth right out!

And I'm finally gonna get my name on the Big Tooth!

CHAPTER 5

Get Ready...
Get Set...

I walked back to class and sat down in my chair to finish the math worksheet. I could feel Max's eyes staring at me, so I turned and winked at him.

After what seemed like forever, Mrs. Wushy rang her bell and said, "OK, boys and girls, it's time for recess. Please hand me your papers, and then you may go out."

I jumped up, handed Mrs. Wushy my paper, and bolted toward the door.

Robbie grabbed my arm and yanked me back before I reached the door. "Hey! Where are you going?" he asked.

"Let go of me!" I said, trying to shake my arm loose. "I'm going to fight Max."

"Are you crazy?" Robbie knocked on my head. "Hello. Anybody in there? The biggest bully in the whole first grade is about to kick your butt, and you're going out there?"

"Yeah."

"What?"

"Yeah. And he's gonna punch me right in the mouth and knock my tooth out! Then I'll get to sign the Big Tooth, just like you!"

"That's so stupid."

"No it's not."

"Yes it is! I think I'd better go tell Mrs. Wushy."

"Oh no you don't," I said, making a fist. "Or I'll knock *your* teeth out!"

Robbie shook his head. "Stupid, stupid, stupid."

"No! This is my lucky day! Now, are you coming or not?" I ran out the door with Robbie at my heels.

"Wait, wait!" he yelled.

"What now?"

"Good luck."

"Thanks!"

"You're gonna need it!"

Just then, Max came running across the yard. "Well, lookie here. The Big Chicken finally came out of hiding."

"I wasn't hiding. I was just getting ready."

"Bock, bock, bock," Max clucked as he strutted around the yard, flapping his arms like a chicken.

"I'M NOT A CHICKEN!" I yelled.

Jessie poked Robbie. "What's Freddy doing?"

"He's gonna fight Max."

"Really?" said Jessie. "How brave."

"Did you hear that?" I turned to Robbie. "She thinks I'm brave."

"Not brave, just really dumb," Robbie muttered under his breath.

"Hey, everybody come over here!" yelled Jessie. "Freddy's gonna fight Max."

The whole class gathered around us in a big circle, pushing and shoving to get a good view of what was about to happen. I squeezed my lucky shark tooth, hoping for some extra power.

"Hey, Freddy's gonna fight Max! Freddy's gonna fight Max!" they all whispered.

Max rolled up his sleeves and started cracking his knuckles in preparation.

All the kids started chanting, "Fred-dy, Fred-dy, Fred-dy."

"Come on, *Tiburón*! You can do it!" yelled

Jessie as she hopped back and forth and punched the air like a boxer.

"Hey, watch my hair, Jessie," said Chloe, fluffing her bouncy red boing-boings. "My mom spent an hour curling it this morning."

"Well, *excuuuuse* me, you little fancy-pants. It's just hair!"

"Well, you're just jealous," said Chloe as she walked away with her nose in the air.

"Whatever."

"This is crazy!" Robbie mumbled.

"I know. Isn't it great?" Jessie said to Robbie. Then she turned and screamed, "LET'S GO, FREDDY! SHOW HIM WHAT YOU'VE GOT!"

I gulped hard. "Just think of the tooth. Just think of the tooth," I whispered to myself.

CHAPTER 6

The Fight

The chants of "Fred-dy, Fred-dy, Fred-dy" were ringing in my ears.

"It's now or never," I thought.

"Hey, Dog Breath!" I yelled, pointing at Max.

"What'd 'ya call me, Baby Teeth?"

"You heard me, Dog Breath," I said, putting up my fists and jumping around. "Come on! Come on!"

Max made a fist, raised his arm high above his head, and started to swing.

I squeezed my eyes shut, took a deep breath, and stuck out my jaw.

I could already see myself signing the Big Tooth.

Then, WOOMPH! Right . . . in . . . the . . . stomach.

CHAPTER 7

Hard, Crunchy Things

Max was sent to the principal's office.

I was sent to the nurse.

And worst of all, I still had all my teeth.

Bummer. I guess that wasn't such a great plan after all.

After school, I was going to play at Robbie's house, so we rode the bus together.

"I still can't believe you got in a fight with Max Sellars. That was really stupid!"

"No it wasn't."

"Yes it *was*!"

"Well, I really want to lose a tooth."

"Too bad you're not a shark in real life, Freddy. You know, sharks lose their teeth all the time."

"Thanks for the lesson, Einstein, but I already know all about shark teeth. As soon as they lose one, another tooth grows in. Some sharks go through sixty thousand teeth in their lifetime. Isn't that amazing?"

"Well, there are other ways to lose a tooth," said Robbie.

"I can't think of any other ways."

"Well, I ate a lot of hard, crunchy things like carrots and apples. Then one day my tooth got wiggly, and I wiggled it and wiggled it every day."

"Did it work?"

"I lost my tooth, didn't I?" Robbie said, pointing to the hole in his mouth.

We had reached Robbie's house, so we ran inside, dropped our backpacks, and went straight to the kitchen to get a snack.

"Mom, we're home!" Robbie called.

Mrs. Jackson came into the kitchen. "Hello, boys. What's up?"

We both looked at each other with that "If you don't tell, I won't tell" kind of stare that best friends have and answered together, "Nothin'."

"Did anything exciting happen today?"

"Nah. Same old stuff."

"Well, you must be starving. What do you want for a snack?"

"Do you have any carrots, Mrs. Jackson?"

"Carrots? Freddy, are you on a diet?" she said, chuckling. "Sorry, I'm all out. That's on my grocery list for this week. What else can I get you?"

"How about an apple?"

"Nope. I put the last one in Kimberly's lunch today. I know," said Mrs. Jackson. "How about some Berry Blast Jell-O?"

Jell-O! Rats! I wouldn't lose any teeth eating Jell-O. That's what they give to babies and old people who don't have any teeth!

"No, thanks," I said. "I'm not that hungry."

"Suit yourself," said Robbie. "I'll have some Jell-O, Mom."

I watched Robbie eat his purple Jell-O and stared at the hole in his mouth as he took each bite.

"It's just not fair," I thought. "I'm three months older than he is."

When Robbie finished, we went to his room to play.

"What should we play? Wanna do some experiments with my new chemistry set?"

"Naw, I'm not in the mood."

"Wanna go outside and catch roly-polies and look at them under my microscope?"

"Naw."

"I know. Let's play with Rosie and Violet."

I shook my head. Rosie and Violet were Robbie's pets, a ball python and a leopard gecko.

"Well, what *do* you want to play?" Robbie sighed, exasperated.

"I don't know." I shrugged.

"You're no fun today."

"You know what? I'm just gonna go home. I'm tired."

"Whatever, party pooper."

"See ya. I'll call you later."

"I may not be around, because we're going out to a special dinner to celebrate me losing my first tooth."

Tooth, tooth, tooth. If I heard that word one more time, I was going to scream!

CHAPTER 8

I Give Up

I walked around the corner to my house, opened the door quietly, and started up the stairs to my room. I really didn't feel like talking to anybody.

"Well, look who's here. Mighty Mouse."

I looked up to see my sister staring down at me.

"How's your stomach feel, big boy?" she asked, laughing. "Oh, I just wish I could have been there to see it. That must have been hilarious! I bet he barely touched you, and you just crumbled like a cookie."

"How do you know about the fight?" I asked nervously.

"Oh, good news travels fast. It was all over school."

"Please don't tell Mom and Dad," I begged. "I'll do your chores for a week."

"Too late. Mom already knows."

"Thanks a lot!"

"It's nothing."

Just then, my mom appeared at the top of the stairs. "Freddy? I didn't hear you come home."

"You're going to get it now," my sister whispered into my ear.

"Freddy, we need to talk," said my mom.

My stomach started doing flip-flops.

"Right now? I'm . . . uh . . . really . . . uh . . . tired. I just want to go to my room."

"Yes, now. Come on." She grabbed my hand. I tried to wriggle free, but she was holding my fingers so tight I thought she was going to crush my pinkie. There was no getting out of this. She led me down the hall to my bedroom. My sister followed us in there.

"Suzie, you need to go finish your homework."

"Oh, that's OK. I can finish it later."

"No, you can finish it now," my mom said, giving Suzie another one of her Death Stares. "Good-bye."

"Yeah, toodles," I said, waving.

She slammed the door and stomped down the hall.

"Freddy, Suzie told me you got in a fight at school today. Is that true?"

I stared down at my toes.

"Freddy, I am asking you a question, and I expect an answer."

"Ymmm," I mumbled.

"What was that? I couldn't hear you."

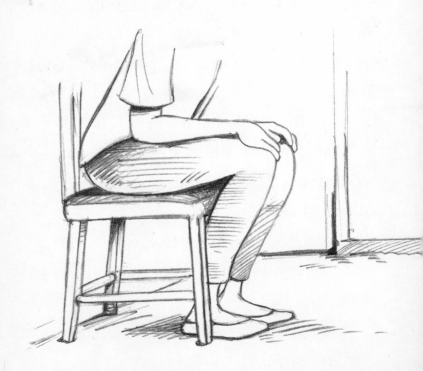

"Yes!" I shouted, as the tears started welling up in my eyes.

"Why?"

I began sniffling. "I'm the only one. . . . Max called me a baby. . . . He was teasing

me. . . . I really wanted to lose a tooth. . . .
I wanted him to knock my tooth out.
Please don't be mad."

"Oh, Freddy," my mom said, laughing.
"I'm not mad."

"You're not?"

She wiped a tear off of my face. "No, I
understand."

"You do?"

"Yes. Sometimes when we want something really badly, we do silly things. But I
hope you learned your lesson. And please
promise me that will be your last fight."

"I promise."

"And I promise you *will* lose a tooth. How
about if we go out for ice cream when your
dad comes home? I bet a little Chocolate
Banana Rama would cheer you up."

"Thanks, Mom."

CHAPTER 9

Is That a Nut?

We got into the car and started driving to my favorite ice-cream place in the whole world, Chilly Willy's.

"How come Freddy is getting ice cream?" said my sister. "He got in a fight. Shouldn't he be getting punished?"

"Be quiet! You're not my mom," I said.

"Well, it's not fair."

"Everything in life isn't always fair," said my mother.

"You always say that," my sister whined.

"Enough, Suzie," said my dad.

"Fine, let the wimp have his ice cream," Suzie said as she stuck her tongue out at me. "You could never have beaten Max, you big chicken!" she whispered as she clucked softly in my ear. "You think that those shark shirts make you look tough, but you really couldn't hurt a guppy."

"Mom, Dad, Suzie stuck her tongue out at me!"

"Suzie, you stop that this instant, or there will be no ice cream for you!"

Suzie turned and gave me her most evil stare, but I just smiled back and gave her my "Oh, I'm so cute" grin.

As we pulled into the parking lot, I saw the dancing ice-cream cone out in front of the store. It's really a guy dressed in an ice-cream suit who hands out free samples.

"Ooooh, I wonder what yummy flavor he has today?"

"Your favorite," Suzie said. "Mushed-up gopher guts with a cherry on top."

"Hello," said the cone. "Would you like to try Nutty Buddy today?"

"No, thanks. I don't like nuts, especially in my ice cream."

"Well, we've got lots more flavors for you inside."

We went inside, and I looked in the cases. "Hmmm, what do I want today—Blueberry Blast, or Chocolate Candy Bits, or Tutti-Frutti?"

"Make a decision, Shark Breath," said my sister. "We don't have all day."

"One more nasty word out of you, young lady," said my dad, "and you're going to wait in the car."

"I'll have a scoop of Strawberry Swirl in a cone, please," I said.

I got my ice cream and sat down in a booth. The ice cream tasted good, and I started to forget about my bad day.

"Feeling a little better?" my mom asked.

"Yeah, I guess, but I still wish I wasn't the only one."

I sat in silence for a while, slowly licking my ice cream.

All of a sudden I felt something hard in my mouth. "EEEWWW! There's a big nut in my ice cream, and I hate nuts!" I did a huge gulp and swallowed it quickly so I wouldn't have to taste it.

"No, *you're* nuts," said my sister. "There's no nuts in Strawberry Swirl ice cream."

"Well then, what did I just swallow, Miss Know-It-All?" I said as I opened my mouth and pointed down my throat.

"Your tooth," she said.

"Ha-ha, very funny," I said.

"No, I'm serious. You just swallowed your tooth!"

"Oh my gosh! It *is* your tooth," my mom said excitedly as she leaned over and gave me a big hug.

"Yep. I can see the little hole in your mouth where it used to be," said my dad.

I looked at them like they were all crazy. "What are you guys talking about? How can I swallow my tooth if I don't have a loose tooth?"

"Not anymore, you don't. You just swallowed it," said my dad.

I shoved my finger in my mouth and started feeling around. Sure enough, there was a little hole right in the front.

"Congratulations, honey," said my

mom. "I know you've been waiting a long time for this."

I jumped out of the booth and started screaming at my family. "WHAT ARE YOU PEOPLE SO HAPPY ABOUT? I JUST SWALLOWED MY TOOTH! MY FIRST TOOTH! NOW THE TOOTH FAIRY WON'T COME, BECAUSE I DON'T HAVE A TOOTH TO PUT UNDER MY PILLOW!"

"Calm down, Freddy," said my dad. "And please lower your voice. People are starting to stare at you."

"Calm down! Calm down! This is the worst day of my life." I fell back into the booth, put my head in my hands, and started to sob.

"Hey, Crybaby," Suzie said, poking me. "You could always leave her a note."

"Huh?" I looked up.

"Leave her a note. Just tell the Tooth Fairy that you're really sorry you don't have a tooth to leave for her, but you swallowed it."

"Do you think that'll work?" I asked, wiping my eyes and nose on my shirt.

"I don't know, but it's worth a try. My friend Sandra said she did that once when her tooth fell out of her pocket at school, and the Tooth Fairy took her note and left some money."

I threw my arms around her and gave her a big hug. "You're the best sister in the whole world."

"I know," Suzie said.

CHAPTER 10

Dear Tooth Fairy...

As soon as we got home from Chilly Willy's, I ran upstairs and started digging through the piles of junk in my room for a piece of paper. I finally found a piece under my bed and licked a smudge of chocolate off one corner.

"There, good as new. Now I just need to find a pencil."

I grabbed one out of my backpack and
sat down on my bed to think. I was about
to start writing when I remembered that I
really didn't know how to spell very well.

"SUZIE!" I yelled.

I heard her footsteps in the hall. "What?"

"Can you help me write this letter to the Tooth Fairy? I need you to tell me how to spell the words."

"What's in it for me?" Suzie asked.

"I'll give you my snack money for a whole week."

"It's a deal," she said, and we locked pinkies. "Pinkie swear?" she said.

"Pinkie swear," I said.

"OK, what do you want to say?"

I wrote the letter, and Suzie told me how to spell the words.

Dear Tooth Fairy,
I'm really really sorry there's no tooth under my pillow. I

swallowed it by accident. Can you please leave me some money anyway? I promise to leave a tooth next time. Thank you very very much!!!

Love,

Freddy Thresher

"Thanks, Suzie."

"Sure. Just remember, I get your snack money tomorrow."

"I remember. Good night."

"Good night."

Suzie left the room, and then I carefully folded up the letter and stuck it under my pillow.

"Oh, I hope she comes," I whispered to my stuffed animals—Bobo, Buster, and Bananas.

CHAPTER 11

The Big Tooth

The next morning when I woke up, I carefully slid my hand under my pillow and felt something cold and round. I threw my pillow on the floor. The note was gone, and there in its place was a big, beautiful, shiny silver dollar!

"Woo-hoo!" I hollered, jumping up and down on my bed. "Today's my lucky day!"

When I got to school, I ran into the classroom and almost knocked Robbie over.

"Hey, watch it," he said. "What's the big hurry?"

I was jumping around yelling, "I'm not the only one! I'm not the only one!"

Mrs. Wushy came over. "My goodness, Freddy, calm down. You almost knocked all our library books on the floor. What are you so excited about?"

"Now I'm not the only one!" I shouted, hugging her.

"What do you mean, 'not the only one'?" Mrs. Wushy asked.

"Now I'm not the only one who hasn't lost a tooth. My tooth fell out last night."

"I didn't know you had a loose tooth," said Mrs. Wushy.

"Neither did I," I said, "but it fell out last night when I was eating ice cream, and I swallowed it!"

"You did?" said Jessie. "Are you OK?"

"Oh yeah. I'm fine."

"Too bad you didn't have a tooth for the Tooth Fairy," said Robbie.

"She came anyway."

"She did?"

"Yeah. I just wrote her a note, and told her I swallowed it, and she left me a big, shiny silver dollar."

"Well, congratulations," Mrs. Wushy said, giving me a hug. "Boys and girls, come to the rug. Freddy lost a tooth last night, so he's going to sign the Big Tooth."

"Sign the Big Tooth." Those words were music to my ears. It was finally my turn to sign the Big Tooth. I had waited for this day for a long time.

I strutted to the front of the room, took the special pen with the smiling tooth from Mrs. Wushy, and signed my name. REALLY BIG.

F-R-E-D-D-Y.

DEAR READER,

I have been teaching children for fifteen years, and on the wall of my classroom I have a big tooth just like the one in Freddy's classroom. My students are so excited when they lose a tooth because they get to write their names on that big, white tooth.

A lot of kids actually lose their teeth at school. I remember one time a little boy swallowed his tooth while he was eating a peanut butter and jelly sandwich! He had to write a letter to the Tooth Fairy and tell her that his tooth was in his stomach. Another time, I had to dig through the sand because a little girl lost her tooth while she was making sand castles at recess.

I bet you have a funny tooth story of your own. I'd love to hear it. Just write to me at:

Ready, Freddy! Fun Stuff
c/o Scholastic Inc.
P.O. Box 711
New York, NY 10013-0711

I hope you have as much fun reading *Tooth Trouble* as I had writing it.

HAPPY READING!

Abby Klein

Freddy's Fun Pages

FREDDY'S
SHARK JOURNAL

There are more than 350 different kinds of sharks in the world.

Most sharks do not hurt people.

My favorite is the thresher shark.
  It can grow to be up to 20 feet long.
  It eats small fish.
  It has a long, powerful tail.
  It doesn't bother people much.

If people knew more about sharks, I don't think they'd be so scared of them. They are really very beautiful.

A VERY SILLY STORY
by Freddy Thresher

Help Freddy write a silly story by filling in the blanks on the next two pages. The description under each blank tells you what kind of word to use. Don't read the story until you have filled in all the blanks!

HELPFUL HINTS:

A **verb** is an action word (such as run, jump, or hide). An **adjective** describes a person, place, or thing (such as smelly, loud, or blue).

One day,_____ and I were playing in the
  a friend

_____. We were _____
  a place   a verb ending in –ing

a _____ when suddenly I tripped over a
  a thing

_____ _____. I landed flat on my
  an adjective   a thing

_____ , and when I stood up, _____
  a body part   the same friend

said, "Look! Your _____ fell out!"
                    the same body part

92

We_____ into the _____
a verb ending in –ed   a different place

to find a mirror, and sure enough, my _____
the same body part

was missing. Just then, I realized . . . it was *really*

missing! We ran back to the_____
the place on page 92

and looked all over the_____. It was_____
a thing   an adjective

so my_____ got a little_____.
a piece of clothing   an adjective

I_____until I was very_____,
a verb ending in –ed   an adjective

but I still couldn't find my_____.
the same body part

That night, I told_____ what happened.
a person

_____ told me to put a_____ under my
The same person   a thing

pillow for the_____Fairy, so I did. The next
a silly thing

morning, when I woke up, the_____ Fairy
the same silly thing

had left me two_____ _____!
an adjective   things

JESSIE'S TOOTH PILLOW

If you want to make a cool tooth pillow like mine, follow these simple directions.
—Jessie

1. Cut out the patterns on the opposite page. You can trace them on to a piece of paper and then cut the paper. Like Jessie, you can also make them larger.

2. Trace smile shape #1 on to two pieces of red felt.

3. Trace smile shape #2 on to a piece of white felt.

4. Glue the white smile on to one of the red smiles.

5. Using a black permanent marker, draw lines on the white smile to make teeth.

6. Cut out a square of black felt the same size as one of the teeth. Put glue on three sides of the black square and glue it on top of the white tooth, leaving it open at the top so it makes a pocket. (This is where you will put the tooth you lost!)

7. Put some stuffing in between the two red

smiles and have an adult glue or sew the two pieces together to make a little pillow.

8. Put your tooth inside the pocket, put the tooth pillow next to your head, and wait for the Tooth Fairy!

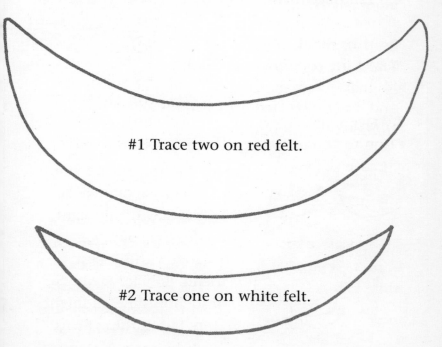

#1 Trace two on red felt.

#2 Trace one on white felt.

Freddy has *another* problem— a really, really, big problem!

FREDDY THRESHER almost never has anything cool for show-and-tell, but this time he's found something amazing. How will he sneak it past his "Neat Freak" mom and bring it to school?

Read all about it in *The King of Show-and-Tell*!

And don't miss Freddy's hilarious adventures in *Homework Hassles*. . . .

Freddy has to write a report on a nocturnal animal. So why not stay up all night and do some outdoor research with his best friend, Robbie? Freddy's ready for some midnight fun, but nothing turns out the way it's planned!